Dedicated to my two boys. I will always be proud of you. — Your dad

Sign up for news, giveaways, and book companion lesson plans at www.piccopuppy.com. Follow us @PiccoPuppy on Instagram and Facebook. #iwillalwaysbeproudofyou #michaelwong #piccopuppy

A special thank you to my wonderful team: Zina Iugai (illustrator) and Brooke Vitale (editor).

Font Credits

Lost Brush by Stripes Studio

Century Schoolbook by Morris Fuller Benton

Marck Script by Denis Masharov

Copse by Dan Rhatigan

Cormorant Upright by Christian Thalmann

Josefin Sans by Santiago Orozco

First published in 2022 by Picco Puppy

Marketing Munch Pty Ltd DBA Picco Puppy, PO Box 103 Killara NSW 2071 Australia

Picco Puppy is a registered trademark of Marketing Munch Pty Limited

ISBN 978-1-922638-49-6

I Will Always Be Proud of You

MICHAEL WONG   •   ZINA IUGAI

I look at you, my *Benjamin*,
and feel a sense of pride.

The love that grows inside my heart
is one I cannot hide.

One day, I know you'll spread your wings,
and then you will fly free.

Today I watch you, *Benjamin*,
and wonder what you'll be.

Will you enrich our souls with wondrous music or wise words?

Will you protect our animals—
our mammals and our birds?

Perhaps you'll captivate the world
with stunning works of art,

Or cook the most delightful meals
that help to warm the heart.

Will you rush into danger so
that you can save the day,

Or nurse the sick to health again
so that they all may play?

It may be, *Benjamin*, that you will
help those who need aid,

Or coach all kinds of athletes so
they'll reach their highest grade.

Perhaps you will empower kids
to be all they can be.

Or *Benjamin*, you just might save
the creatures of the sea.

Will you one day discover how
to cure the common cold?

Or maybe you'll show kindness that
is valued more than gold.

It might be that you'll turn our waste
to something that has worth,

Or pioneer clean energy
to make a healthy Earth.

Will you turn your thoughts, *Benjamin*,
to what waits in the stars?

Or will you build a wonderful
new world for us on Mars?

Your passion waits, my *Benjamin,*
so find the truest you,

And strive to be the best you can
in everything you do.

When clouds of doubt turn sunshine to
a dark and hazy gray,

Stay strong and know tomorrow
always brings a brighter day.

I have no doubt you'll reach your dreams
and get there without fear.

Just know that if you need me,
Benjamin, I'll be right here.

I wish you happiness, no matter
what you choose to do.

I love you and . . .

I always will be

very proud of you!

Can You Spot the Famous People?

Benjamin, no matter what obstacles you face, believe in yourself and all that you are—just like these famous people did. Can you spot all five in the book?

Can you spot a young Annie Jump Cannon?

Annie Jump Cannon was born in 1863. She was a pioneer in the field of astronomy. Cannon classified about 350,000 stars by their spectral characteristics (temperature, color, size, brightness, and composition).

Can you spot a young Bessie Coleman?

Bessie Coleman was born in 1892. In 1921, she became the first African-American woman and Native American to earn a pilot's license. She was known as "Brave Bessie" for doing dangerous stunts at air shows.

Can you spot a young Friedrich Fröbel?

Friedrich Fröbel was born in 1782. At the time, children under the age of seven did not attend school. Fröbel's belief that young children should be educated changed that. In 1837, he opened the first "kindergarten."

Can you spot a young Ludwig van Beethoven?

Ludwig van Beethoven was born in 1770. He is one of the greatest composers of all time. Amazingly enough, Beethoven wrote some of his greatest works after going deaf. His music is still popular today.

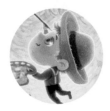

Can you spot a young Vincent van Gogh?

Vincent van Gogh was born in 1853. He is a famous painter, known best for *Starry Night* and *Sunflowers*. Van Gogh did not start painting until he was 27. He painted about 900 paintings in ten years.

Can You Spot the Dogs?

There are 22 dogs in the book. *Benjamin*, can you spot them all?

Bernese Mountain Dog

Bichon Frise

Border Collie

Brussels Griffon

Bulldog

Cairn Terrier

Cane Corso

Chesapeake Bay Retriever

Chihuahua

Chow Chow

Cocker Spaniel

Collie

Coton de Tulear

Dachshund

Labrador Retriever

Miniature Schnauzer

Old English Sheepdog

Rottweiler

Russell Terrier

Samoyed

Scottish Terrier

Shih Tzu

We hope you enjoyed the book.
Please support us by rating the book on Amazon. It will help me
write more books. Please also share on social media. Thank you.
Sign up for giveaways and lesson plans at www.piccopuppy.com.

Michael Wong is an award-winning children's author.
He is passionate about creating empowering, diverse,
and inclusive books for kids. Michael lives with his wife
and two children in Sydney, Australia.

Zina Jugai is an artist who fills her illustrations with
light and atmosphere. She dreams of creating magical
worlds with her illustrations.

I Wish You Happiness, Benjamin

MICHAEL WONG • ANN BARATASHVILI

Also by Michael Wong, *I Wish You Happiness, Benjamin*.
Available on Amazon and PiccoPuppy.com.

Made in the USA
Middletown, DE
07 December 2022